Disney PRESENTS A **PIXAR** FILM

THE INCREDIBLES

THE MOVIE STORYBOOK

Adapted by Louise Moore

Illustrated by the Disney Storybook Artists

Designed by Kristen Johnson of Disney Publishing's Global Design Group

Inspired by the art and character designs created by Pixar Animation Studios

Random House 🏠 New York

Copyright © 2004 Disney Enterprises, Inc./Pixar Animation Studios. All rights reserved under International and Pan-American Copyright Conventions. Published in the United States by Random House Children's Books, a division of Random House, Inc., New York, and simultaneously in Canada by Random House of Canada Limited, Toronto, in conjunction with Disney Enterprises, Inc. RANDOM HOUSE and colophon are registered trademarks of Random House, Inc.

The term OMNIDROID used by permission of Lucasfilm Ltd.

Library of Congress Control Number: 2004107718

ISBN: 0-7364-2269-2

www.randomhouse.com/kids/disney

Printed in the United States of America
10 9 8 7 6 5 4

During the golden age of Supers, one hero stood out among the rest. With the sharpest crime sense in Municiburg, he used his Super strength to capture villains and protect innocent citizens from unfortunate disasters. He was even known to have rescued one cat from the branches of a tree while using the very same tree to stop some escaping crooks. In a word, he was *incredible*! That's right, folks. We're talking about . . .

Mr. Incredible!

There were other Supers, too—heroes like Frozone, that cool dude who could freeze villains instantly; Gazerbeam, whose laserlike vision sought out evildoers; and Mr. Incredible's personal favorite, the lovely Elastigirl. This amazing rubbery woman could stretch across vast expanses to knock unsuspecting villains silly. Each of these crime fighters was superb. But when Mr. Incredible was on the job, he never allowed a single one to fight by his side.

"I work alone" was his well-worn response.

Ordinary citizens idolized the Supers. One boy named Buddy dared to dream of being Mr. Incredible's sidekick. This number-one fan even called himself Incrediboy and invented a pair of rocket boots to help him fly—but it was all in vain. Supers were born, not made.

One evening, Buddy showed up at a crime scene to "help" Mr. Incredible fight the notorious Bomb Voyage. He flew out the window to get the police . . . but didn't realize that one of Bomb Voyage's explosives was attached to his cape!

"Buddy! Don't—"

cried Mr. Incredible. He grabbed on to Buddy and tore off the bomb, saving the boy. But the bomb plummeted to the ground and destroyed some train tracks in a loud explosion. The hero quickly stopped an oncoming train on the very brink of disaster. Once again, Mr. Incredible had saved the day!

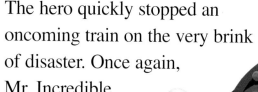
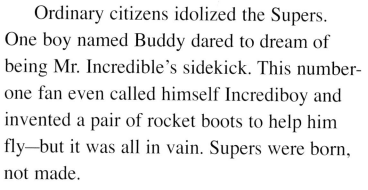

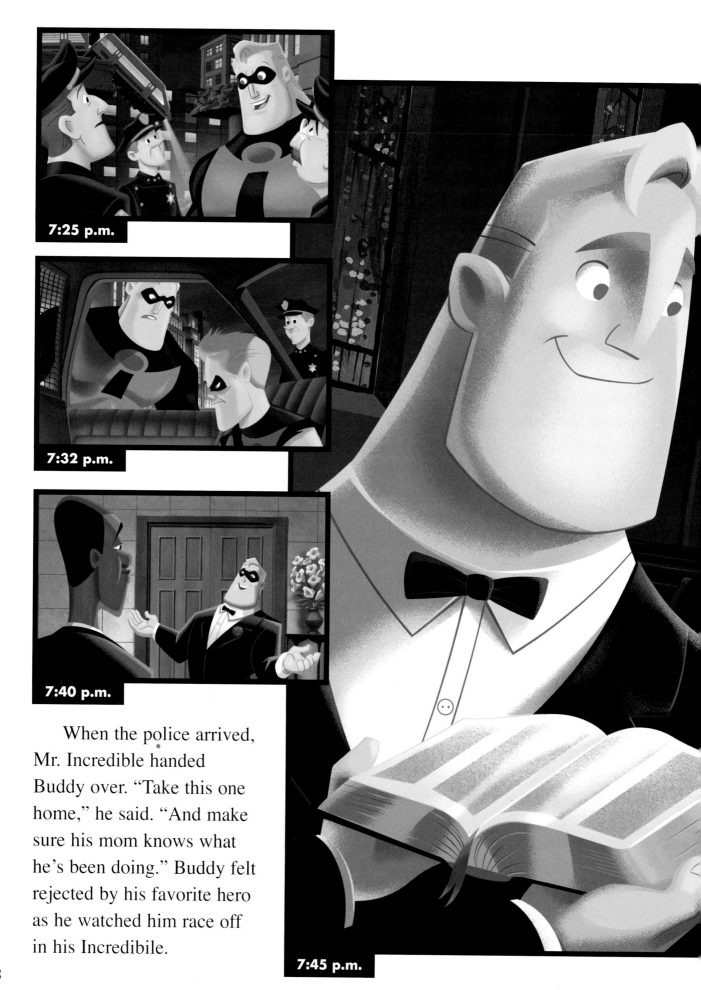

7:25 p.m.

7:32 p.m.

7:40 p.m.

When the police arrived, Mr. Incredible handed Buddy over. "Take this one home," he said. "And make sure his mom knows what he's been doing." Buddy felt rejected by his favorite hero as he watched him race off in his Incredibile.

7:45 p.m.

Mr. Incredible's timing was perfect. Not only did he save many lives that day, he also managed to arrive in the nick of time to marry his lovely bride—Elastigirl! All the Supers were in attendance on that glorious day. It was the height of **a golden era . . .**

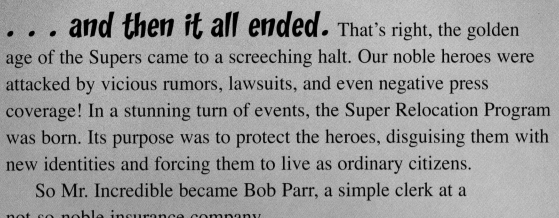

. . . and then it all ended. That's right, the golden age of the Supers came to a screeching halt. Our noble heroes were attacked by vicious rumors, lawsuits, and even negative press coverage! In a stunning turn of events, the Super Relocation Program was born. Its purpose was to protect the heroes, disguising them with new identities and forcing them to live as ordinary citizens.

So Mr. Incredible became Bob Parr, a simple clerk at a not-so-noble insurance company.

But life was rarely boring or normal for Bob's Super family.

At dinner one night, Elastigirl (now known as Helen Parr) was feeding baby Jack-Jack—the only family member without Super powers. Jack-Jack's older brother, Dash, began to tease their shy sister, Violet. Like normal siblings, Dash and Violet argued. Unlike normal siblings, they had Super powers. Dash had lightning speed, while Vi was able to turn invisible and create force fields.

Helen tried to stop the fighting by wrapping herself around the entire family. She looked to her husband for help, but the former Mr. Incredible was distracted. He was reading in the newspaper about his old hero friend Gazerbeam.

"Bob?" Helen cried. "I need you to intervene!"

"Okay!" said Bob, lifting his tangled family, table and all.

"I'm intervening!"

Just then, the doorbell rang. It was Lucius Best—formerly known as Frozone. After telling Helen they were going bowling, Bob and Lucius sat in a parked car and listened to a police scanner for any trouble. Suddenly, they heard a report of a building on fire.

"Yeah, baby!" shouted Bob. He wanted to save people!

But Lucius was reluctant. "We're gonna get caught."

Bob didn't hesitate. He charged toward the burning building. Lucius followed. Neither of them noticed a mysterious woman watching from the shadows.

To protect their identities, Bob and Lucius put on ski masks. Then the two former heroes raced through the burning building, rescuing people as they went. Nothing could stop them . . . until Lucius became dehydrated. He couldn't use his freezing powers.

"What?" cried Bob.

"You're out of ice?"

Bob was forced to smash through a brick wall to escape the burning building. Unfortunately, they wound up in a jewelry store and set off the alarm system. BEEP! BEEP! BEEP! Alas, being a hero was not always easy. A police officer was on the scene in an instant. Were the two heroes about to be arrested?

Luckily, Lucius managed to reach for a cup of water! He was Frozone once again and quickly put the officer on ice. The two masked heroes escaped into the dark of the night, leaving the frozen copsicle behind.

Overall, Bob figured, it had been a pretty good night. He had saved people, and he hadn't gotten caught—that is, until he got home, where Helen was waiting for him.

"Is this . . . RUBBLE?"

she asked as she stretched her arm across the room.

"It was just a little workout, to stay loose," Bob said, trying to defend himself.

"You know how I feel about that, Bob! We can't blow our cover again," complained Helen.

"I performed a public service. You act like that's a bad thing."

"Uprooting our family again because you had to relive the glory days is a very bad thing!" Helen argued.

"Hey, reliving the glory days is better than acting as if they didn't happen!"

Bob couldn't help it. He couldn't let go of the past.

But Bob knew Helen was right. The next day at the office, he was called in to see his boss. Mr. Huph was angry at Bob for actually helping clients.

Suddenly, Bob's old crime sense kicked in. There was a mugging going on right outside Huph's office!

"That man out there needs help!"

Bob said. He was desperate to leap to the rescue. But Mr. Huph wouldn't let him.

"He got away," a frustrated Bob muttered as the mugger ran off.

"Good thing, too. You were this close to losing your j—" But Mr. Huph didn't get the chance to finish. Bob had heard enough. He tossed Huph . . . who ended up flying through five office walls.

Bob was fired. Again.

Wondering how to ask his family to move yet again, Bob returned home and retreated to his den to reflect on the good old days. That was when he found a tiny computer hidden inside his briefcase.

"Hello, Mr. Incredible," said a woman on the screen. "My name is Mirage. Yes, we know who you are. Rest assured, your secret is safe with us. We have need of your unique abilities. If you accept, your payment will be three times your current annual salary."

Bob was suspicious but definitely intrigued. With this job, he could be a **HERO** again! (And he wouldn't have to tell Helen he had been fired.)

The next morning, Bob told Helen he was going to an out-of-town work conference. Secretly, he dressed in his old Super suit (which was a tad too tight) and boarded an ultrasleek jet bound for the island of Nomanisan.

"The Omnidroid 9000 is a top-secret prototype battle robot. Its artificial intelligence enables it to solve any problem it's confronted with," Mirage began, briefing Mr. Incredible on his assignment. "And unfortunately—"

"Let me guess," said Mr. Incredible. "It got smart enough to wonder why it had to take orders. You want me to shut it down without completely destroying it." He was on a roll. He felt his old hero instincts kicking in.

Mirage was impressed. **"You _are_ Mr. Incredible,"** she said with a sly smile.

Moments later, our hero was air-dropped
into the jungle. This would be a tough mission:
he had to outsmart a robot designed to outsmart
him . . . and he was in less than top Super shape.

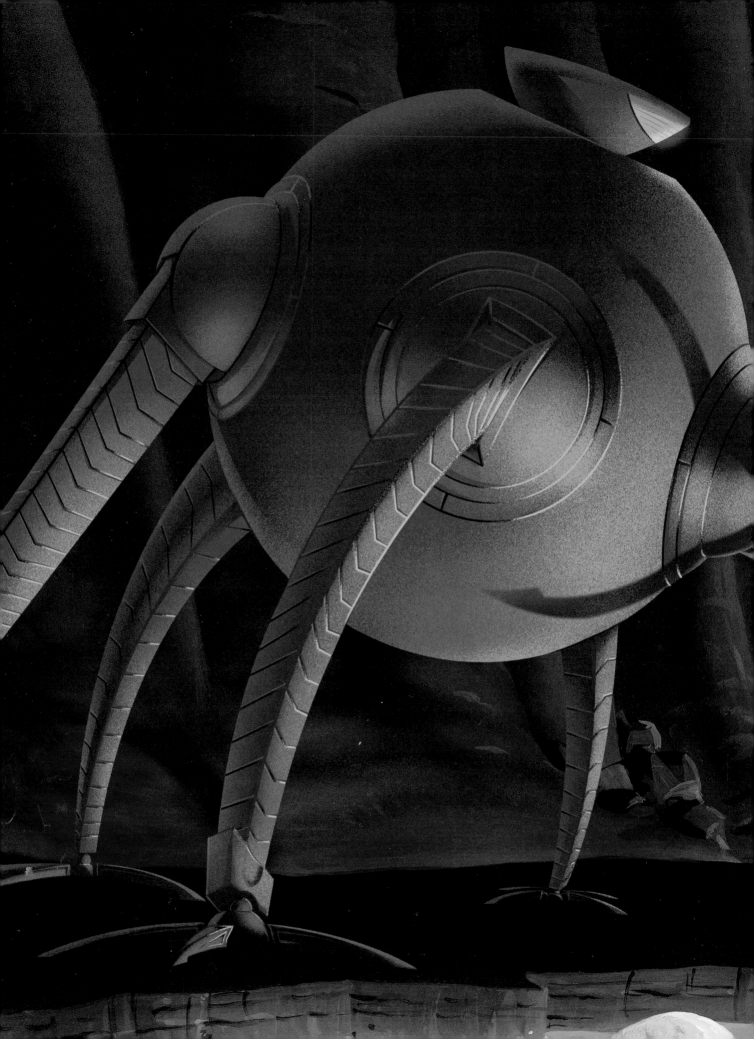

Mr. Incredible ran through the jungle, then stopped to listen. He whirled around when he heard a crunching metallic sound. There it was—**the Omnidroid!** The giant hunk of steel with robotic spider legs waged a mean battle. It smashed and bashed Mr. Incredible until he finally climbed inside the robot, disabling it. With the Omnidroid lying crumpled at his feet, our hero took a moment alone to relish his success.

But was he truly alone? Mirage watched on a computer screen, with a mysterious man right by her side. . . .

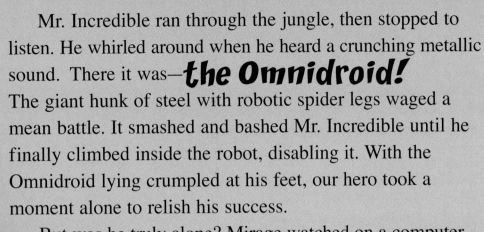

Bob returned home a new man. He bought a new sports car for himself and a car for Helen, too. He played football with Dash and hung out with Vi. He flirted with his wife and took his turn feeding Jack-Jack. He even regained his top Super shape by working out at the train yard.

But there was one small problem: Bob had not yet told Helen that he had lost his job at Insuricare—and that he had returned to work as

Mr. Incredible!

"Hurry, honey, or you'll be late to work!" Helen called out one morning as Bob stuffed his Super suit into his briefcase. Bob cringed. How long could he keep this secret from Helen? But there was no time to worry. He was off to see . . .

... EDNA MODE! Bob had torn his Super suit in the battle with the Omnidroid, so he was visiting the world's greatest fashion designer, affectionately known as E, to get it fixed. E had been the top designer of Super suits before heroes were forced underground. She was thrilled to be working with a Super again. But simply patching Bob's old suit was not enough.

"You need a new suit," declared E. **"It will be BOLD. DRAMATIC! HEROIC!"**

"Yeah. Something classic, like Dynaguy," agreed Bob. "He had a great look. The cape, the boots—" **"NO CAPES!"** interrupted E. Too many heroes had gotten tangled in their capes, leading to terrible accidents. For sentimental reasons, E also agreed to repair Bob's old suit.

Soon Mr. Incredible was back at Nomanisan, sporting his new Super suit. Suddenly, a new and improved Omnidroid attacked him. The terrible robot was just about to end Mr. Incredible's heroic life when a strange man appeared . . . the same man who had secretly watched him defeat the first Omnidroid. Mr. Incredible quickly recognized him. It was Buddy, the kid he had saved years earlier. Ever since that fateful day when Mr. Incredible had ended Buddy's dream of being Incrediboy, Buddy had grown more and more bitter toward Mr. Incredible—and all the other Supers. Now he invented evil, destructive machines.

**"I am Syndrome!
Your nemesis!"**
shrieked the maniacal
grown-up Buddy.

With a wicked laugh, Syndrome tossed Mr. Incredible in the air with his immobi-ray invention. Mr. Incredible fell off a cliff and into a river. Had Syndrome finally witnessed the demise of his ex-hero? To be sure, the evil villain sent a robot probe into the water . . . and it confirmed that

Mr. Incredible was dead!

Well, not really. In an underwater cave, Mr. Incredible had hidden behind the skeleton of the missing hero Gazerbeam. And Gazerbeam had left a valuable clue: he had used his laser vision to burn the word

KRONoS

into the cave wall.

Back home, Helen noticed that a tiny rip in Bob's old Super suit had been repaired. She knew that only one person could patch a true Super suit. Helen raced over to E's mansion.

"You helped my husband resume secret hero work behind my back?" cried Helen when it was clear to her that Bob had been lying.

"I assumed you knew, darling," E responded. Then she proceeded to show Helen the Super suits she had created for the entire Parr/Incredible family. E also told her about the **homing device** attached to Bob's Super suit. One push of the button and Helen would know where to find him. . . .

Meanwhile, on Nomanisan, Mr. Incredible had infiltrated Syndrome's lair. At the main computer, he typed in the password:

KRONOS

It worked! But Mr. Incredible was shocked by what he found. Almost all his heroic friends from the glorious golden age were gone—destroyed by Syndrome and his evil inventions! It was all part of Syndrome's plot to use his machines to make himself the one and only "hero" left on Earth.

Worried about his wife, Mr. Incredible frantically searched the computer for Helen's Super name. At last it popped up on the screen:

ELASTIGIRL: LOCATION UNKNOWN

Mr. Incredible sighed with relief. Helen was okay! But suddenly a mysterious beeping sound came from his suit. . . .

Sure enough, Helen had just activated the homing device. Instantly, Syndrome's high-tech security system picked up the signal and zeroed in on the hero. Mr. Incredible raced down a long hallway, only to be pummeled by giant squishy blobs of goo. There was no escaping now. **Mr. Incredible was trapped!**

After discovering the location of her husband, Helen knew she had to help him. She took her family's Super suits from E and went home to pack.

Later, zooming through the skies in a jet, Helen left the cockpit briefly to change into her Super suit. Elastigirl was ready for action! And so were . . . Dash and Vi? That's right, the Incredible children had found their Super suits and followed their mom.

"You left Jack-Jack alone?"

Elastigirl cried.

"Of course we got a babysitter, Mom! Do you think I'm totally irresponsible?" asked Vi.

Elastigirl was still worried, but there was no time to change plans—the jet was under attack!

Back on the island, Syndrome was very angry.

"Who did you contact?" Syndrome demanded, wondering about the homing device. Mr. Incredible didn't know what he was talking about. Then Mirage played the radio transmission of a plane requesting permission to land: "Island approach, India Golf Niner Niner checking in. . . ."

"Helen!" Mr. Incredible gasped, recognizing his wife's voice.

"So you do know these people," said Syndrome. "Well then, I'll send them a little greeting." With a malicious grin, he fired rockets at the plane.

Syndrome's computer quickly confirmed the worst:

TARGET DESTROYED.

Mr. Incredible's family was gone! He grabbed hold of Mirage.

"Release me!" he commanded. "Or I'll crush her."

"Go ahead," replied Syndrome with a sneer.

But Mr. Incredible could not bring himself to hurt Mirage. Defeated, he let her go.

Not far away,
Mr. Incredible's family was alive!

Elastigirl had shaped her elastic body into a parachute and lowered her children safely to the ocean. Then she took the form of a boat, and Dash's powerful legs became the kicking motor. When they made it to shore, Elastigirl quickly found a cave where Dash and Vi could hide.

"I think your father is in trouble. I'm going to look for him," she said. Then she reached inside her duffel bag and pulled out their three Super masks.

"Put these on. Your identity is your most valuable possession," Elastigirl said. "Protect it. If anything goes wrong, use your Super powers."

Elastigirl raced through the jungles of Nomanisan to Syndrome's headquarters. Searching and stretching through the corridors, at last she found her husband . . . hugging Mirage?! **KAPOW!** Elastigirl's fist flew across the room and punched the mysterious woman right in the jaw.

What Elastigirl didn't know was that Mirage had just released Mr. Incredible and told him his family was still alive! Mirage had abandoned all loyalty to Syndrome when the evil genius had challenged Mr. Incredible to crush her.

"She was helping me escape!" Mr. Incredible tried to explain.

"No, that's what *I* was doing," Elastigirl snapped back.

But the argument was cut short when Mirage told them that Dash and Vi had triggered a security alert. Syndrome's guards were chasing them!

Indeed, Dash and Vi were using their Super powers to escape Syndrome's guards at that very moment. They were awesome, terrific, and, yes, **INCREDIBLE!** But even incredible kids have a hard time fighting a whole ton of bad guys. Just as things were looking bleak, Mr. Incredible and Elastigirl arrived to save the day! Together, the family fought off Syndrome's guards until—

"WHOA! WHOA! WHOA! TIME OUT!"

Syndrome cried, appearing suddenly. Within moments, the Incredible family was suspended in midair, imprisoned by Syndrome's immobi-ray. Would they ever escape Syndrome's clutches? Would this be the end of the Supers?

Back at headquarters, Syndrome revealed his evil plan to the imprisoned family. After setting the Omnidroid loose on Metroville, he planned to go to the city and defeat the robot, passing himself off as a Super!

He would be the greatest hero ever!

Mr. Incredible watched in despair as Syndrome left to put his plans in action.

"I'm so sorry I got you all caught up in this," Mr. Incredible said to his family.

Then something incredible happened. Vi used her force field to escape the immobi-rays— and free the entire family!

Mirage helped the Incredibles get to Metroville in a van attached to a rocket. They landed on the freeway at 200 miles per hour and screeched to a halt downtown.

Mr. Incredible wanted to work alone.

"I can't lose you again!" Mr. Incredible told his wife. "Not again. I'm not strong enough."

"If we work together, you won't have to be," Elastigirl said gently.

And so our noble Super family set out to
destroy the Omnidroid—together!

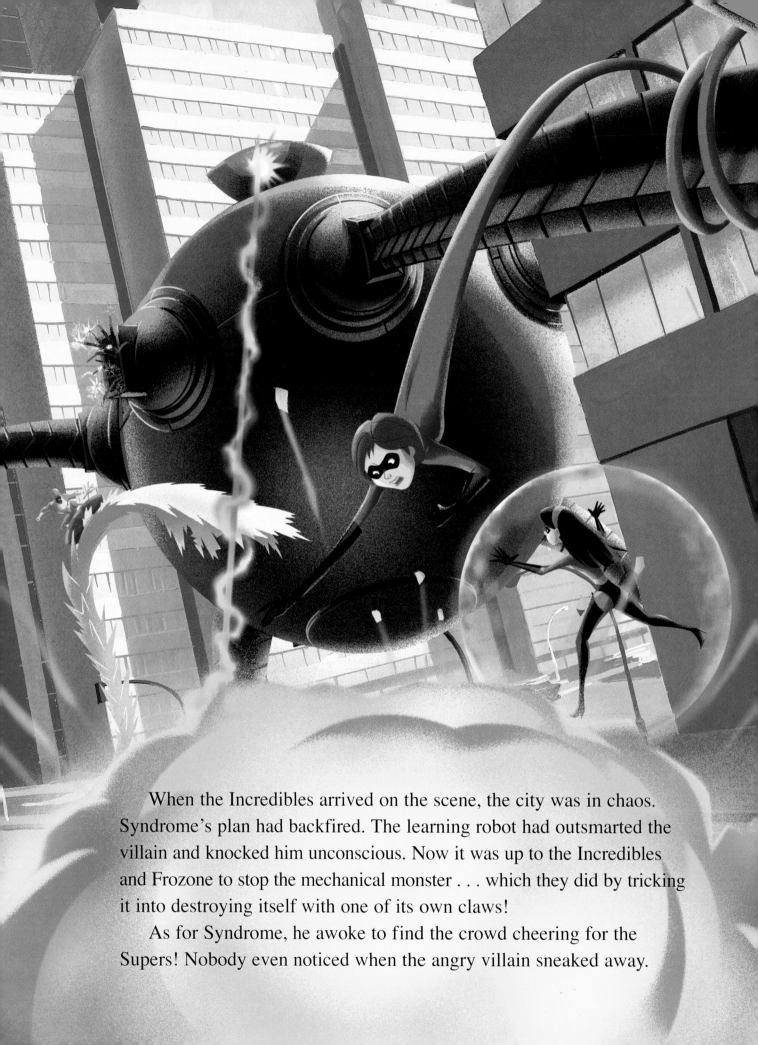

When the Incredibles arrived on the scene, the city was in chaos.
Syndrome's plan had backfired. The learning robot had outsmarted the
villain and knocked him unconscious. Now it was up to the Incredibles
and Frozone to stop the mechanical monster . . . which they did by tricking
it into destroying itself with one of its own claws!

As for Syndrome, he awoke to find the crowd cheering for the
Supers! Nobody even noticed when the angry villain sneaked away.

The crowds cheered the glorious return of the Supers. Afterward, the Incredibles were shuttled home—heroes once again.

But at home, the heroes found Syndrome waiting for them. Grabbing baby Jack-Jack, the villain flew through the roof toward his waiting jet.

"You stole my future. I'm returning the favor," he taunted them.

But luckily, Jack-Jack had Super powers after all—he transformed into a mini-monster! Terrified, Syndrome released the baby. And that's when the Incredibles sprang into action! Elastigirl caught Jack-Jack and parachuted him safely to the ground. Then Mr. Incredible threw his sports car at Syndrome's jet, destroying the villain's means of escape. The heroic family was victorious, and Syndrome was never heard from again!

And so the Incredibles returned to their undercover life. Only this time, normal life wasn't that bad. Dash was allowed to run on the track team . . . as long as he agreed to always come in second. And as for Vi, well, she was a little less shy. All that rescuing had empowered her to face her greatest fear—boys!

Yes, our heroes had returned to normal life. Well, sort of. After all, a Super's life is never completely normal . . . especially when a villain could be waiting right around the corner.